ALAN the WRENCH
WELCOME to WORKINGTON
"A - Z"

Visit Alan the Wrench in Workington
to have more fun while learning:

www.alanthewrench.com

Facebook:

https://www.facebook.com/AlanTheWrench

Twitter:

https://twitter.com/AlanTheWrench1

Instagram

https://www.instagram.com/alanthewrench1

This book is dedicated to the child in all of us. Don't ever let anyone tell you what is and what is not possible. That is for you to decide. This book is also dedicated to my loves Elena, Jojo, Jakers, and Jules, or they would be angry at me for not mentioning them.

Alan the Wrench

Tool type: Allen wrench

Alan the Wrench is the hardest-working tool in all of Workington. He is an assembler at the largest furniture company in town. He has a wife named Alison Wrench and three kids. His oldest daughter is Alyssa Wrench, who is 14. Alan the Wrench Jr is 10, and his little sister Alana Wrench is 7.

Bob Plumb

Tool type: Plumb bob

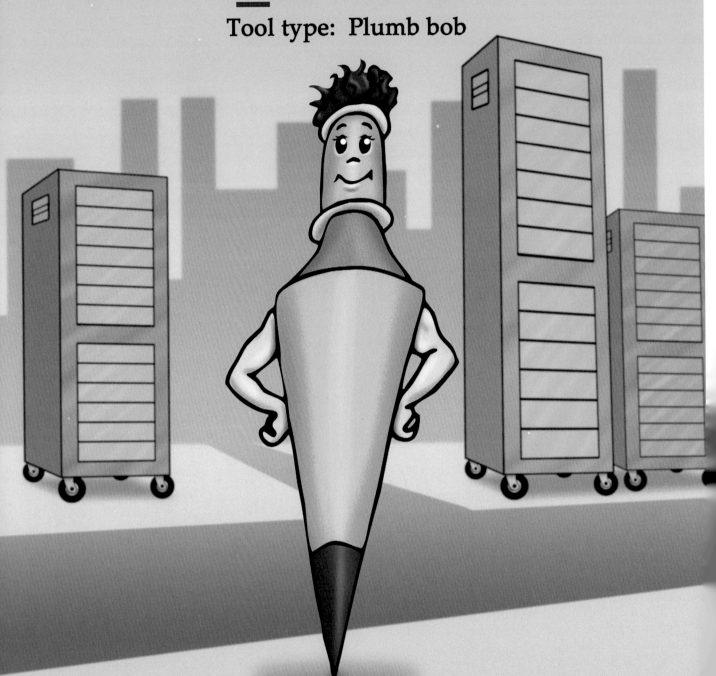

Bob Plumb has been Alan the Wrench's best friend since kindergarten. Bob helps keep things straight and level, working for the Workington Construction Company. He builds tall skyscrapers and cozy homes.

Chip Chizler

Tool type: Chisel

Chip Chizler drives the town garbage-and-recycle truck in Workington. He is great when it comes to keeping the streets of Workington clean.

Doctor Charles Lox

Tool type: Groove joint pliers

Dr. Lox is Workington's finest physician who tends to the needs of all the citizens in town. He can fix a broken handle, tighten a big bolt, loosen a rusty nut, and much much more!

Ethel Clampett

Tool type: C - clamp

Ethel Clampett is the Branch Manager for the Workington Savings Bank. She makes sure the bank is running tight and efficient. She greets all bank customers by showing her friendly smile.

Fred Blocker

Tool type: Block plane

Fred Blocker is the owner of the barber shop, Working Over Hair. This is where Alan the Wrench gets his haircut. Fred can do any style, but he's best when you tell him, "Take a little off the top."

Gunnar Cutt

Tool type: Backsaw

Gunnar Cutt owns Workington's largest car dealership and is very proud of his Nordic heritage. His car dealership slogan is "We are Gunnar Cutt prices in half!"

Hank Hammah

Tool type: Ball-peen hammer

Hank Hammah runs the local hardware store, The Tool Box. If you need supplies to build, fix or restore a project, Hank Hammah's store will have it.

Ivanna Weeders

Tool type: Garden tool

Ivanna owns the most beautiful Workington florist studio, which is called Blossoms. She loves working in her garden growing all kinds of fruits and vegetables.

Jack Hammah

Tool type: Sledgehammer

Jack Hammah is the Gym Teacher at Workington Elementary School. He likes blowing his whistle during gym class. The kids all love Mr. Hammah because he always plays their favorite games in gym class.

<u>K</u>eenan Shackleton

Tool type: Hacksaw

Keenan Shackleton is a stand-up comedian and performs at The Rusty Nail comedy club. He tells corny dad jokes that really aren't that funny. However, the food is good at the club.

Lance Niveau

Tool type: Level

Lance Niveau is from France and owns Workington Furniture Company. He is Alan the Wrench's boss. Niveau means "level" in French.

Molly Plyars

Tool type: Needle-nose pliers

Molly Plyars is Lance Niveau's secretary at Workington Furniture Company. She went to high school with Alan the Wrench and Alison Wrench.

<u>N</u>eil Sett

Tool type: Nail set

Neil Sett is the former Welterweight Boxing Champion of the World. He now owns the Workington boxing gym, Tough As Nails.

Officer Lenny Leinmann

Tool type: Lineman's pliers

Officer Leinmann is a Police Officer who helps keeps Workington safe and sound. In his free time, he loves listening to country music and playing with his dog, Otto.

Piper Kuttah

Tool type: Pipe cutter

Hard work = freedom!

Miss Kuttah is a schoolteacher at Workington Elementary School. She is Alan the Wrench Jr's favorite teacher because she makes learning fun!

Quentin Ratchet

Tool type: Ratchet

Quentin is a talented musician who can plan any instrument. Everyone in Workington calls Quentin by his nickname, "Q."

<u>R</u>usty Niffe

Tool type: Glass razor scraper

Workington's oldest citizen can often be found in the
park feeding the birds. He tells great stories of when
Workington was founded.

Scotty Staples

Tool type: Staple gun

Scotty Staples is Alan the Wrench's good friend, even though they are the complete opposites. Scotty drives the town school bus, and the kids all love him.

Tim Shares

Tool type: Tin shears

Tim Shares is owner of the largest plumbing company in Workington, Hot and Cold. He makes sure everyone has heat in the winter and air-conditioning in the summer.

Ursula Prunez

Tool type: Hand pruning shears

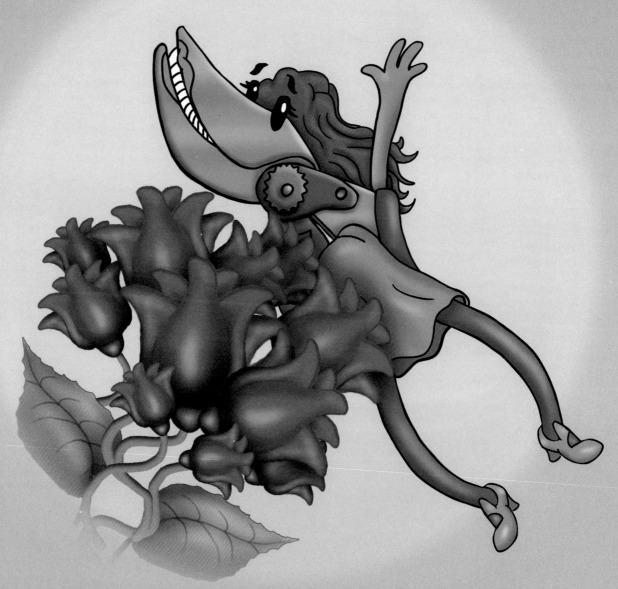

Ursula Prunez is owner of the largest landscaping company in town, Ultimate Landscaping. She keeps all of Workington looking beautiful and colorful with all kinds of flowers.

Vic Grippz

Tool type: Vise grips

Vic Grippz is the Mayor of Workington. He makes sure Workington is in perfect working order. He relies on all the tools in town to work together to make sure Workington is a safe and happy place.

Wendy Diggs

Tool type: Gardening tool

Wendy Diggs runs the Workington Country Club and
Golf Course. She is the town golf champion.

Xavier "Speedy" Square

Tool type: Speed square

Xavier Square is an architect who is also known as "The X-Man" by everyone in Workington. He keeps everything in town on the straight and narrow path.

Yannis Grecco

Tool type: Y-type wrench

Yannis Grecco runs the most popular delicious pizza-and-submarine-sandwich shop, YNOT's. YNOT is TONY spelled backward. Tony is Yannis's dad's name.

Zachary "Zippy" Lein

Tool type: Zip tie

Zachary makes sure everything and everyone is grounded and secure. Nothing blows away when Zippy is around!

PROJECT COMPLETED

Made in the USA
Middletown, DE
19 January 2019